ADVENTURES AT HOUND HOTEL

a Capstone company — publishers for children

Raintree is an imprint of Capstone Global Library Limited, a company incorporated in England and Wales having its registered office at 264 Banbury Road, Oxford, OX2 7DY – Registered company number: 6695582

www.raintree.co.uk
myorders@raintree.co.uk

Edited by Jill Kalz
Designed by Heidi Thompson
Original illustrations © Capstone Global Library Limited 2017
Illustrated by Deborah Melmon
Production by Tori Abraham
Originated by Capstone Global Library
Printed and bound in China.

ISBN 978 1 474 72060 1 (paperback)
20 19 18 17 16
10 9 8 7 6 5 4 3 2 1

British Library Cataloguing in Publication Data
A full catalogue record for this book is available from the British Library.

Cool Crosby

by Shelley Swanson Sateren

illustrated by Deborah Melmon

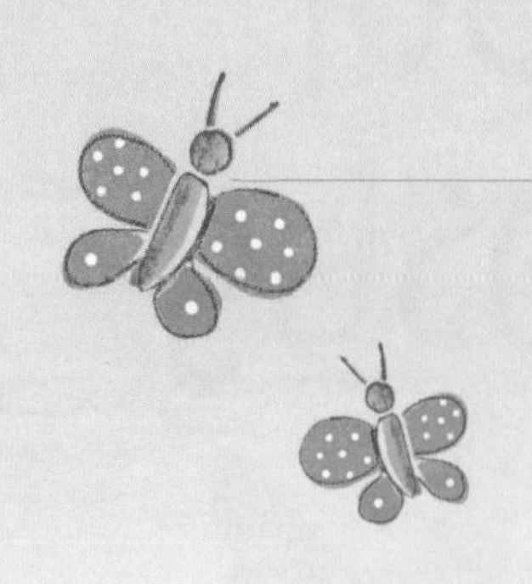

CONTENTS

ADVENTURES AT HOUND HOTEL

IT'S TIME FOR YOUR ADVENTURE AT HOUND HOTEL!

At Hound Hotel, dogs are given the royal treatment. We are a top-notch boarding kennel. When your dog stays with us, we will follow your feeding schedule, take them for walks and tuck them into bed at night.

We are just a short walk away from the dogs – the kennels are located in a heated building at the end of our driveway. Every dog has his or her own kennel, with a bed, blanket and water bowl.

Rest assured . . . a stay at the Hound Hotel is like a holiday for your dog. We have a large paddock plenty of toys and a pool for the dogs to play in, in the summer. Your dog will love playing with the other guests.

HOUND HOTEL WHO'S WHO

WINIFRED WOLFE

Hound Hotel is run by Winifred Wolfe, a lifelong dog lover. Winifred loves all types of dogs. She likes to get to know every breed. When she's not taking care of the canines, she writes books about – that's right – dogs.

ALFIE AND ALFREEDA WOLFE

Winifred's twins help out as much as they can. Whether your dog needs gentle attention or extra playtime, Alfreeda and Alfie provide special services you can't find anywhere else. Your dog will never get bored whilst these two are helping out.

WOLFGANG WOLFE

Winifred's husband helps out at the hotel whenever he can, but he spends most of his time travelling to study packs of wolves. Wolfgang is a real wolf lover – he even named his children after pack leaders, the alpha wolves. Every wolf pack has two alpha wolves: a male wolf and a female wolf, just like the Wolfe family twins.

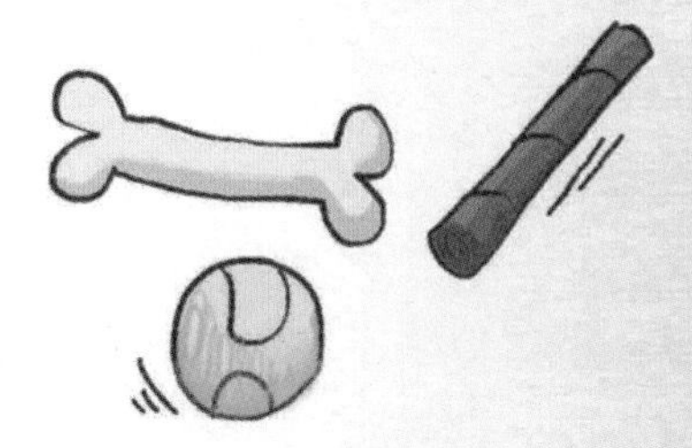

Next time your family goes on holiday, bring your dog to Hound Hotel.

Your pooch is sure to have a howling good time!

CHAPTER 1

The world's most annoying brother

I'm Alfie Wolfe, and there's one thing I hate: when my twin sister, Alfreeda, acts like the alpha kid around our place. "Alpha" means "first" or "top."

She's always wiggling her finger in my face and telling me what to do. *So* annoying!

But this story isn't about the most annoying sister in the world. Well, not totally. It's about the world's most annoying brother.

You see, there's this German shepherd I know. His name is Crosby. He's stayed at Hound Hotel before, and he is the coolest dog ever. Crosby's super strong and friendly and can jump really high. He loves to leap over stuff and race around outside.

The problem is, he's got a little brother – a puppy called Bruno. Bruno is a brat with a capital B. Trust me, both he and my sister are alphas in the annoying department.

Sometimes Alfreeda makes me so angry that my head almost explodes. That's when I start to yell and kick stuff. Then I'm in the doghouse. That means I'm in trouble with Mum and Dad.

But back to Crosby. I never felt sorrier for a dog. He had to put up with Bruno. Every. Single. Day.

It all started early one morning back in June. I groaned and hit the button on my dog clock to make it stop barking.

Suddenly, my sister marched right into my room, without even knocking. I *hate* it when she does that!

"Get up, sleepyhead," she ordered me in her top-boss voice.

"Get out of my room," I said, rolling over against the wall. Against a poster hanging on the wall, to be exact. Against a poster my dad had given me, to be exacter. A poster of a grey wolf, to be exactest.

I stared at the powerful-looking wolf and sighed. I wished I could act more like an alpha wolf – the leader of the pack – around my sister.

But that role was all hers. Between me and her, she always came out stronger, smarter, braver and faster. In every area. It wasn't fair.

Now Alfreeda marched over and whipped off my blanket.

"Two more dogs just checked in, Alfie," she said. "The hotel's full. With Dad up north at the Wolf Centre, Mum needs our help. She said we're supposed to speed through our chores. Then we're supposed to play with the dogs so they're not bored. I call dibs on Crosby."

"Huh?" I sat up super fast. "Crosby? The German shepherd?" I asked. "The one who was here last month?"

Alfreeda grinned. "Yep. He's back. And I get to play with him today. It's my turn. You hogged him last time. You can play with the beagles who checked in yesterday. Or the terriers. Or the Labs."

"No!" I leaped out of bed. "*I* call Crosby."

Alfreeda laughed. "Sorry, Alfie. I'm already dressed. I've had breakfast. And now I'm going to do my chores. Mum says whoever finishes their chores first gets to play with Crosby. Crosby *and* Bruno, that is."

"Broon-who?" I asked.

"Bruno," she said. "Crosby's new little brother. A German shepherd puppy. He's *so* cute! He and Crosby are staying in the same pen, just for tonight. I get to play with both of them because *I'll* speed through my chores. Unlike you, slowcoach."

She grinned again and ducked out of my room. I ran after her and tripped over the big stuffed wolf Dad had given me.

"I get Crosby!" I cried. "I'll make a great obstacle course for him, just like last time!"

"Too late, sleepyhead," Alfreeda called from downstairs. "I've got all kinds of fun stuff planned for Crosby."

"*You?*" I yelled. "No way!"

Our back door slammed.

I quickly took off my pyjamas and threw on jeans and a Hound Hotel T-shirt. Then I ran downstairs and gobbled up my breakfast in record time.

I raced down our long driveway to the kennel building. I just *had* to spend all day playing with Crosby and his brother. Crosby was the coolest dog around.

I'd build the best obstacle course Crosby had ever seen. I'd make his stay at Hound Hotel the most fun ever. The best country holiday he'd ever had!

But first I had to do my kennel chores.
If I was going to beat my sister, I had to save time in the chores department.

CHAPTER 2
Little red riding nonsense

So how could I finish my chores before my sister finished hers? Maybe fill the dogs' water buckets only half full? Maybe sweep just a little bit of the dog hair from the pens?

Maybe Mum wouldn't notice. Ha! Fat chance of that. Mum was famous for her spotless kennels. That was a big reason dog owners kept coming back to our hotel.

But here was another reason: Dogs had loads of fun at Hound Hotel, thanks to us twins. We loved to play with the dogs. So I *had* to build a super-cool obstacle course for Crosby.

I threw open the kennel building's front door. "Mum!" I called. "Can I play with Crosby first? He'll have loads more fun with me. That's just as important as chores, right? Hey, Mum, where are you?"

I ran through the office and down the hall, towards the big room at the back of the building. That's where the pens are. Or you can call them kennels. You can even call them runs, if you want. Why runs? Because each space is big enough for a dog to *run* around inside it. Get it?

I ran past the laundry room door just as Mum stepped out. She carried a basket piled high with clean, folded laundry.

BAM! I crashed right into her.

Towels and blankets flew into the air. They fell to the floor, totally unfolding themselves.

Oops.

"Alfie, you *know* you're not supposed to run in here," Mum said with a groan. "Well, *I'm* not folding these again. That will be *your* job. Lay them neatly on the storeroom shelves when you're finished." She shook her head and started to walk away.

"What?" I cried. "On top of my other chores? I'll *never* get to play with Crosby at this rate! *Ugh*!" I kicked a pile of clean towels. They flew back into the air. One landed on Mum's head. She pulled it off, turned around and stared at me.

"Alfie," she said in her I'm-warning-you voice. "Control your temper. Understand?"

"Yeah. Sorry," I said. "But it's not fair. Alfreeda always gets to play with the best dogs because she's super fast at chores. And super good at getting up earlier than me. I'll *never* be the alpha kid around here – at *anything*."

"Oh, Alfie," Mum said, patting my shoulder. "Of course you will. Honestly, the way you and your sister fight over being number one is completely silly – it's just silly. Silly! You are equal to your sister in many areas. Even tops in others."

"Name one, Mum."

At that moment her mobile phone barked. (Our phones don't ring, they bark.) "Hold that thought, Alfie," she said. "Excuse me."

She answered her phone and started talking in her regular normal voice. She wandered into the office and shut the door.

I sighed and flopped onto the floor. I got busy folding the stupid laundry. It took forever. I. Am. Not. Kidding.

Finally I got the piles put away in the storeroom. I ducked into the kennel room and looked around. Exactly half of the dogs' drinking-water buckets were full of fresh water. Half of the pens looked swept. Half of the dog dishes were full of food. Of course Alfreeda had left half of the morning chores for me.

And of course she'd finished her share at alpha-kid speed. My sister annoyed me.

Alfreeda was kneeling in Crosby's pen, patting his noble-looking head. My heart felt a tug. I wanted to be with him so badly!

Then I noticed Bruno the puppy. He was chewing Crosby's tail. He chewed and chewed on it, like it was a tasty, treat-filled toy.

The pup wouldn't stop. Crosby wagged his tail out of Bruno's mouth a few times. But every time, the pup jumped back and chewed like mad again.

I doubt it hurt, but it must have really annoyed him. I bet Crosby wanted to snap at his bratty little brother. Only he couldn't. Because Alfreeda held his head in her hands.

She spoke to him in her talking-to-babies voice. I *hate* when people talk to dogs like they're toddlers. See, here's the thing: Every kind of dog in the world came from wolves. Every dog's great-great-great- (add a lot more "greats" here) grandparents were wolves. Would you talk to a wolf in baby talk?

If your answer is no, here's a high five. If your answer is yes, I feel super sorry for your dog.

Now Alfreeda rubbed her nose against Crosby's. Gross! Sister germs! Poor guy.

"You German shepherds look *so* much like wolves, don't you?" she said in that weird baby voice. "Your bushy tails. Your pointy ears."

She kissed him on top of his head. More sister germs – double gross! How could Crosby stand it?

"Well, guess what?" she squeaked. "Because you look *so* much like Mr Wolf, we are going to put on a play. Yes! Right here in your pen. We'll spend all morning right here, playing theatre. Won't that be *fun*?"

Crosby looked at the floor. He yawned.

"Exactly," I said. "He doesn't want to stay inside. He wants to be outside, in the sun, running around."

"Be quiet, Alfie." Alfreeda rolled her eyes. "This is none of your business. Do your chores, and leave us alone."

I groaned and started to fill water buckets. Out of the corner of my eye, I peeked at Crosby's pen. Now Bruno was jumping on Crosby's tail, over and over. Like he was trying to squash it flat. Crosby didn't even whimper.

"So Crosby," Alfreeda continued, "do you want to know the title of the play?"

She moved his head up and down, making him nod.

"*Little Red Riding Hood*," she said. "I'll be Little Red. You'll be the wolf in a granny suit. Bruno will be the loaf of bread. He'll lie in a basket, nice and still. I'll carry him through the woods to Granny's house. Won't doing a play be fun?"

"No, it won't," I piped up. "Crosby doesn't want to put on some dumb *Little Red Riding Nonsense* play. He won't ever want to come back to Hound Hotel."

"Yes, he will," Alfreeda said.

"No, he won't!" I argued. "Now that he's got that little brat in his life, Crosby needs an extra-great holiday. He needs to do action-y fun stuff, not quiet stuff. You're totally ruining his sleepover!"

"Am not," my sister said.

"Are too!" I said.

My face got super hot. I wanted to kick something. Hard. I tried to kick my sister, but instead, I kicked over Crosby's full bucket of drinking water. Water splashed everywhere.

"Mum!" Alfreeda cried.

Oops.

Lost my temper again.

CHAPTER 3
In the doghouse

The second Alfreeda cried out like a big baby, Mum came running.

For a long time, Mum just studied me and the mess I'd made.

Water had soaked Crosby and Bruno's beds. Afreeda's shoes and jeans too. It dripped off the dogs' fur. There were puddles in Crosby's kennel and the pen next door. The only dry thing around was me.

I was clearly in the doghouse.

But lucky for me, Mum never yells around our hotel guests. She wants the hotel to be a calm place for our visitors. Alfreeda and I are never allowed to yell in the kennel building either, no matter how angry we get at each other. (Yelling makes dogs nervous, just like it makes people nervous.)

Mum brought me a mop.

"Get busy, Alfie," she said. "Alfreeda, take dry bedding to the laundry room for Crosby and Bruno. Play with them in there until their pen is dry. I'll be in the paddock with the other dogs. I'll need both of you to help with the lunchtime feeding."

I spent about ten minutes all by myself, mopping up. It was lonely, I can tell you. I wished Dad were there. But then again he would have made me clean up my mess too.

I needed some cheering up.

I needed Crosby.

Slowly I laid down the mop and then crept up the hall. I couldn't believe my good luck. Alfreeda hadn't shut the laundry room door all the way. It stood open just a crack.
I peeked inside.

Crosby lay on his bed beside the tumble dryer. Bruno sat on top of Crosby's head and chewed his brother's ear. Chewed his ear!
I. Am. Not. Kidding.

With a sigh, Crosby gently shook Bruno off his head. The puppy slid onto the bed with a soft *plop*.

And guess what! Bruno climbed right back up Crosby's neck. He sat on Crosby's head again and got busy chewing Crosby's *other* ear.

Crosby growled a little – a low growl. But that was it. He never lost his temper.

Did Alfreeda notice all this? No! She was biting her lip and cutting up a big cardboard box. She laid it flat on the floor and started to paint a forest on it.

That's another one of my sister's abilities that makes me sick: She's the alpha artist in our pack – I mean, family. She's the best artist in our year at school too. She doesn't just whip out a drawing or painting. She spends hours and hours on each one.

Mum loves Alfreeda's paintings of dogs the most. She frames them and hangs them all over our house. So I've got an everyday reminder of how gifted and talented my sister is. And how gifted and talented I am not.

After a minute or so, Bruno jumped off Crosby's head. He hopped towards Alfreeda and bit the paintbrush. He pulled it out of her hand and ran around the room with it in his mouth.

"Hey!" Alfreeda said. "Give that back." She crawled after him, but Bruno kept wriggling out of her reach.

The pesky pup led her in a wide circle. Then he ran right over the freshly painted trees in the fairy-tale forest. He jumped off the cardboard and left a trail of teeny brown and green footprints all over the floor.

That's when Alfreeda cornered him. "No,

you don't. Come here, you," she said.

She wiped his feet with a wet cloth then wiped the floor. Next she plopped the puppy in Crosby's bed. She pushed the pup right between Crosby's front paws.

"Stay, Bruno," she ordered.

Bruno jumped right out.

Alfreeda put him between Crosby's front paws again. This time she crossed Crosby's legs in front of Bruno's nose, like a furry castle wall.

"Hold him right there, Crosby," Alfreeda said. "I'm almost finished painting the background."

Great, I thought. *Now Crosby has to puppy-sit. This is the worst sleepover in dog history! He'll never want to come back to Hound Hotel. His owners will be able to tell that he hates it here. They won't ever send him back, and I'll never see him again. I'll miss him for the rest of my life!*

Bruno tried to wriggle free, but Crosby held him in place. Crosby closed his eyes and sighed heavily.

I was feeling sorrier for Crosby by the second. The two of us could have been outside, racing through the coolest obstacle course ever built. This was all Alfreeda's fault. I could feel my face getting hot again. I think I even started to sweat.

Finally Alfreeda stood the fake forest in front of the washing machine.

"Finished! Now, my fine actors, it's time to try on our costumes," she announced to Crosby and Bruno.

First she wrapped Bruno in a towel and laid him in a basket. "You are a little loaf of bread," she told him. "You have only one thing to do: lie still."

Alfreeda must've wrapped Bruno tight because he didn't even wriggle. He closed his eyes and fell asleep.

"Now it's your turn," she said to Crosby. "You are the star of the show. The wolf in a granny suit."

She reached into a box and pulled out a polka-dotted nightdress and a matching hat. She must've found them in our attic. Maybe they belonged to our great-great-grandma or something. They looked super-old-fashioned.

My heart started to pound. I started breathing fast. My face felt like it was on fire. That strange get-up was the *last* thing a cool wolf-like dog would want to wear!

Alfreeda started to tug the nightdress over Crosby's head. I couldn't keep quiet another second. I had to save him from my sister and her stupid play.

I threw the door wide open. I leaped into the room and shouted, “STOP! Do NOT put those stupid things on him!”

CHAPTER 4

Tug of nightdress

My shout made Alfreeda jump. She fell backwards and bumped her head hard on the washing machine.

"Ow!" She sat up and rubbed her head. "Get out of here, Alfie, or I'm telling."

"No!" I said. "You wouldn't get out of my room this morning."

That shut her up, at least for a second.

Now Crosby wandered around the room with the nightdress totally covering his head.

"Look out, Crosby," I warned him.

Too late. He bumped his long nose right into the wall.

"That's *your* fault," Alfreeda said to me.

"No, it isn't," I said. "You put the thing on him in the first place." I pulled the nightdress off Crosby's head, then patted his nose. "You okay, boy?" I asked.

He licked my cheek.

"Just stick with me, boy," I said. "I'm your man. I'll show you a good time. Come on." I led him to the door.

"Bring Crosby back here," Alfreeda ordered.

"No," I said. "I'm going to talk some sense into Mum. German shepherds are big dogs. They need lots of exercise. They need to run around outside."

"Stop telling me stuff I already know," she said. "It's so annoying when you do that."

"Me? Annoying?" I said. "You're the one who's always acting like a know-it-all!"

"What?" She stuck out her tongue. "*You* always act like a know-it-all!"

"I do not!" I yelled. I stuck out my tongue right back at her. "Would you just stop arguing for once?"

"Me? Argue? Ha! I hardly ever do!" she argued. "But *you* argue ALL THE TIME!"

"DO NOT!" I argued. "Look, Alfreeda, Crosby needs to do some real action-y stuff, not lie around on a stage pretending to be some fairy-tale granny–"

"He'll get out soon enough," Alfreeda said. "Right after lunch–"

"No!" I said. "*Now*. Come on, Crosby. I'm talking to Mum. She knows dogs better than anyone. Especially my sister."

"No!" Alfreeda leaped in my direction. "Let go of him. And give me that nightdress!"

I let go of Crosby's neck fur. He stayed right by my side. Now I held tight to the nightdress. I planned to hide the stupid thing somewhere, like under a big rock beyond a faraway hill.

Alfreeda pulled the nightdress harder.

I pulled it back, towards me, twice as hard.

She gave a stronger tug.

I did too.

Then she pulled it with alpha-kid strength. I almost fell flat on my face.

I straightened up, then gave a crazy-strong yank on those polka-dotted old-lady pyjamas.

"ARRGH!" I yelled.

Alfreeda and the nightdress shot towards me. She stopped herself just before she crashed into my chest.

"Ow!" she said. "You pulled so hard you twisted my arm! It hurts. I'm telling!"

"You pulled hard too!" I said.

"Not as hard as you did." She frowned.

For a second I thought, *I was stronger than my sister for once? Really?*

"Anyway," she said, "you weren't supposed to be in here. You were supposed to be doing your chores. I *am* telling!"

"Don't!" I said.

Alfreeda pushed past me and ran down the hall. She tore through the kennel room and out of the door.

About five seconds later, Mum called from outside. "Alfie! Come here this instant!"

Uh-oh.

CHAPTER 5

Alpha pest of the world

I penned up Crosby and Bruno in the laundry room. Then I dragged myself outside. "Be back soon," I said over my shoulder. "Maybe," I added, swallowing hard.

In the fenced-in paddock, a group of dogs yapped and ran towards me. I kneeled down and gave them lots of chin rubs and pats on the back.

"AL-FIE!" Mum called in her I-mean-business voice.

I sighed and headed to the west-side fence. Mum and Alfreeda were kneeling beside it, hugging a couple of Labs.

Alfreeda saw me coming and started to act like she was out to win a giant acting prize or something. First she stood up all shaky. Next she held out her arm, all loose and floppy-like. Then she bent her neck sideways and did her I'm-dying eyeball roll until her eyes almost disappeared.

"Oh, it hurts *so* much, Mum," she boo-hooed. "I won't be able to do *any* lunchtime chores. I guess I'll just have to play with Crosby and Bruno all day."

I marched right up to Mum. "Give me a break!" I cried. "She's totally faking it! Some of the big dogs pull much harder out on their walks than I pulled just now. Crosby should be outside, playing with *me*! Not inside, cooped up with *her*!"

"Calm down, Alfie," Mum said.

"Impossible!" I cried. "Not when I have Alpha Pest of the World for a sister!"

"Al-fie," Mum warned. "What did I say about controlling that temper of yours?"

I shut my mouth tight but shot Alfreeda the evil eye.

"Listen, you two," Mum said. "No matter how angry you get, you always need to be gentle with each other. Here's one important reason: If either of you gets hurt, we won't have enough workers to run the hotel. Got it?"

Alfreeda and I both nodded.

Mum turned to my sister. "Tell me honestly, Alfreeda," she said. "What's your pain level, between one and ten? One is no pain, ten is horrible pain."

"My pain is an *eleven*," Alfreeda said. "Because *Alfie* caused it."

Mum sighed. "I give up," she said. "Alfie, go and finish your morning chores. Alfreeda, put the German shepherds back in their pen. It should be dry by now. Then finish *Little Red* in there. Alfie, when the play is over, you may take Crosby outside."

"What?" I cried. "But . . . but Alfreeda will drag that stupid play on for *hours* and *hours*. I *know* she will!"

My head was ready to explode. It felt like I had *ten* Brunos chewing on me. All at once!

I swung my leg back . . . gritted my teeth . . . then swung my leg forward . . . super hard. *BOOM!* I kicked a big tub full of dog toys. The tub shot towards the sky and tipped upside down. Balls, Frisbees and chew bones flew everywhere.

"Alfie Wolfgang Wolfe!" Mum cried. "That does it!"

CHAPTER 6

Battle with the brat

It's seriously big trouble when Mum calls my whole name. I had really lost my temper this time. What was I thinking?

Some of the flying balls had hit a few of the dogs on the head.

A Frisbee had hit another dog in the ribs.

The big tub had landed with a *THUNK* right beside a teeny Yorkshire terrier.

(I was *so* lucky the tub hadn't landed on top of him. I shivered just thinking about what could've happened to the little dog.)

Mum swept the scared little terrier into her arms. "It's okay, it's okay," she said. Then she looked at me. Hard. "That was your last chance, Alfie," she said. "You won't be playing with any dogs today, unless you somehow prove to me that you can control your temper. Now pick up these toys. Then go inside and finish your chores."

Without a word I picked up all the toys and dropped them in the tub. I patted the dogs who got hit with balls. I whispered "sorry" to the dog whose ribs got hit with a Frisbee.

Then I ducked indoors. I filled dogs' water buckets super fast. I thought they'd be really thirsty after playing outside. I only spilled a little.

I wiped up the tiny puddles.

After that I got busy sweeping pens.

For about the next half hour, no one spoke. Mum put on some quiet music and started brushing the terriers.

Alfreeda had moved Crosby and Bruno back to their pen. Now she was making a granny house out of another big cardboard box.

She didn't even notice alpha-pest Bruno. But I sure did. Pretty soon I only pretended to sweep dog hair. Instead I kept a watchful eye on poor Crosby.

Bruno had crawled out of the brown towel and hopped out of the basket. He headed straight for his brother and began to chew his bushy tail all over again. Just like it was a tasty morning treat.

Crosby wagged his tail and swept Bruno

away. Then Crosby got up and moved.

Bruno followed.

Now the pup started to bite Crosby's chin. Crosby turned his head away, and Bruno let go.

For a minute, Bruno calmed down a little. But then he started to chew Crosby's front paw. Crosby pulled his paw away. Bruno leaped forward and chewed Crosby's other paw.

Crosby growled, low.

I held my breath. Grown-up German shepherds have really strong jaws. One bite could turn that pup into a tasty snack.

But still the pest didn't stop. Now he started to hit Crosby across the face with his little paw.

Crosby did a deep-gut growl.

Bruno just wouldn't back off. I couldn't believe it! He cuffed Crosby across the face again. And again!

Crosby turned his head away and stared at the fairy-tale forest. Alfreeda was so busy painting the granny house that she didn't notice Crosby's Battle with the Brat.

Then Bruno hopped over and bit Crosby right on the nose.

That's it, I thought. *The pup's a goner. Crosby HAS to lose his temper now!*

But Crosby didn't bite back. He didn't swat his little brother. He didn't snap off his head or even his nose. He didn't howl. Instead, once again, Crosby just turned his head away.

Crosby totally kept his cool. And Bruno got bored. The pup crawled into Little Red's basket again and fell back asleep.

That's when I remembered something Dad once said: All dogs are born with natural instincts – from their wolf kin back in history.

So dogs have lots of the same instincts that wolves do, like hunting, herding and protecting the pack. Another one is called the "calming instinct".

Alpha wolves don't fight with underdogs in their pack, no matter how annoying they are. Why? Because if any members of a pack are wounded, there won't be enough strong fighters to hunt for food. The survival of a pack depends on alpha wolves keeping their cool. Like Crosby.

Here's another thing Dad told me: When the alpha wolf (or dog) turns away and avoids a fight, he (or she) also calms down the pest.

I leaned on the broom and thought more about the "calming instinct." *If alpha-male Crosby, the leader of his little pack, can keep his cool with Bruno the Super Brat,* I thought, *maybe*

I can with Alfreeda. Maybe.

The next time she annoyed me, I'd try to be cool. I'd try to find my calming instinct.

Well, guess what? I got put to the test about two seconds later.

CHAPTER 7

Do the Crosby thing

So there I was, in deep thought about dogs and wolves and their super-cool calming instinct. On the other side of the kennel room, Mum brushed the Yorkshire terrier. Quiet music played. The Hound Hotel was actually pretty peaceful.

Then Alfreeda walked out of Crosby's pen. She shut the gate behind her and marched straight towards me.

“I need to borrow the broom,” she said. “To sweep up cardboard scraps.”

“Go to the storeroom and get your own,” I said. “You know this isn’t the only one.”

“Why should I?” she asked. “You’re not using that one. You’re just standing there, doing nothing.” She wagged her finger in front of my nose and added, “You really should *do* your chores one of these days. Stop being lazy.”

That’s when I dropped the broom. The handle hit the floor with a *BANG*. My hands curled into tight balls, and my temper started to steam inside me like hot soup.

Mum looked up. She dropped the dog brush and put her hands over the little terrier’s ears.

“Alfreeda,” she said. “It’s not your job to tell Alfie what to do. It’s mine.”

Yeah! I thought.

"Now stay calm, Alfie," Mum warned.

That's beyond impossible! I thought, swinging my leg backwards. I was all set to kick Alpha Pest of the World.

But then I remembered Crosby. Cool Crosby.

My leg hung in the air behind me.

I remembered the calming instinct and how it was good for the entire pack. How it could calm down the annoying pest.

I peeked at Crosby. He was staring at me.

Okay, I thought. *I'll do the Crosby thing.* I closed my eyes and took four deep breaths.

I told myself, *Calm down, Alfie. Be cool. You can do it.*

I slowly lowered my leg. I uncurled my fingers and shook my hands loose. Then I turned away from the alpha pest and kept my mouth shut.

I DID it, I thought. *I can't believe I actually did it! Hooray for me!*

I picked up the broom and walked away from my sister. I started to sweep. In no time at all, I had a pile of dog hair ready to dump in the bin.

"Finally," Alfreeda muttered. She headed to the storeroom to get her own stupid broom.

"Well done, Alfie," Mum said, walking over.

"Yeah," I replied. "That's a big pile of dog hair all right."

"I don't mean that." She smiled at me. "I mean, well done for controlling your temper. I know your sister can be annoying sometimes. And I know you annoy her sometimes too. But you proved you can keep your cool and walk away from a fight. *Before* it happens."

Mum patted my shoulder.

Just then Alfreeda marched back, swinging a broom.

"Alfreeda?" Mum said. "I've decided to send Crosby outside to play with Alfie while you finish the theatre set. Crosby really does need some exercise now."

"What?" Alfreeda cried. "But Crosby will forget all about me! I wanted to be his favourite this time! All he wanted to do last time was run through Alfie's obstacle course. Crosby didn't even want to play Frisbee with me.

"It's just not fair," Alfreeda continued. "Alfie always has the best ideas for fun stuff to do, stuff the dogs love. Dogs never like me as much. They always like him more."

She covered her face with her hands.

Wow, I thought. *I never had a clue my sister felt that way.*

Mum put her arm around Alfreeda's shoulders and led her to the laundry room. For a private mum-to-child talk, I guessed.

When I finished sweeping the kennels, I tiptoed into Crosby's pen. Bruno was still asleep in his basket.

"Come on, Crosby," I whispered, leading him out of his kennel. Quietly, I shut the gate behind us. We headed outside.

Once outside I threw my hands in the air and cried, "*Finally*, some fun!"

Crosby barked. Then he tore around in circles at alpha-dog speed.

CHAPTER 8

The coolest obstacle course ever

Crosby kept tearing around in big circles and barking.

It's like he was shouting, "I'm FREE! Free from the pest! A REAL holiday, at last!"

"Just you wait, Crosby," I said. "I'm planning some fun with a capital F. Be right back."

I ran to the garage and dug out a load of stuff: our old slide and paddling pool . . .

a red wagon and a couple of sledges . . . two empty bins and a lot of big old toys . . .

I lugged everything across the driveway and arranged it in zigzaggy rows all over the paddock. I stood the sledges on end and leaned them against the bins.

As the final touch, I filled the paddling pool with water.

"Okay, Crosby." I clapped my hands. "Ready?"

Crosby sat at my feet, panting and grinning.

"This is the coolest obstacle course ever," I said. "A cool course for the coolest dog in the world – *you*!"

Crosby barked and wagged his bushy tail. I rubbed the top of his head.

"Now listen," I said. "You've got the most powerful back legs I've ever seen on a dog.

But if they're rusty, and stuff is too high to jump over, like the sledges, just run around them. Want to walk through the course first?"

He barked and wagged faster.

"Okay," I said, pointing at the obstacles. "First you jump over that . . . then slide down this . . . climb over that . . . jump over this . . . then run around those. Got it?"

Crosby barked and bounced with energy.

"Ready and – *go*!" I cried.

Crosby took off running. He sailed right over the paddling pool without getting a drop of water on a single paw. He didn't even climb the steps of the slide. He just leaped right over the whole thing! Then he cleared the top of the sledges. I couldn't believe my eyes!

"Wow!" I cried and clapped. "Keep going, Crosby! You are amazing!"

Crosby finished the course and started a second lap.

Just then Alfreeda called from the door. "Alfie? Hey, Alfie!"

Go away, I thought. *We're finally having some fun here. Leave us alone!*

I wanted to say those things out loud. But I liked being out of the doghouse better. So I kept my mouth shut.

Still I refused to look at her. This was *my* time with Crosby.

"Alfie!" Alfreeda called again. She marched towards me, then stood right in front of my face. I couldn't even see Crosby.

I was all set to yell *MOVE*, when she held up something.

"Look," she said.

It was a giant ring, cut out of cardboard. Bright yellow and red flames were painted on the edges.

"I made it," she said. "For Crosby to jump through. You can hold it as high as you want. Here. He'll fly right through the ring of fire."

I was super surprised. "Cool," I said. And I meant it.

I took the ring and stood in the middle of the course. I held it high off the ground.

"Hey, Crosby," I called. "Over here! Come jump through this!"

Crosby came sprinting across the paddock, zipping around one obstacle after another. Then he took a flying leap and sailed right through the ring of fire.

"Wow!" I said.

Alfreeda clapped. "Bravo, Crosby!" she cried. "Do it again!"

Right then I realized something: My sister and I were lucky to work at Hound Hotel. We helped make the dogs' visits extra fun. Both of us. My sister *and* me. We had fun too.

"Want to hold it this time?" I offered.

"Yeah!"

Alfreeda held it even higher in the air, and Crosby flew through the ring of fire again.

"Do it again, Crosby Old Boy," I cried.

And he did. Again and again.

At last, fun with a capital F!

HOUND
HOTEL

Is a German shepherd the dog for you?

Hi! It's me, Alfreeda!

I bet you want your own big, strong, bushy-tailed German shepherd now too, right? Of course you do! But actually, German shepherds make good pets for only some families. So before you zoom off to buy or adopt one, here are some important facts you should know:

German shepherds have a strong herding instinct. They get along well with small children or other pets, but look out – they'll herd them around. Grown-up German shepherds weigh about 36 kilograms (80 pounds) and can accidentally knock over a small child. Or step on a teeny pet. So think twice about mixing babies, teeny pets and German shepherds.

German shepherds often have elbow or hip problems. These very painful bone problems make it hard to walk or run. Vets can help. But if you're a family that can't or doesn't want to pay vet bills, then don't get a German shepherd. Or any dog. Get a goldfish instead.

German shepherds shed. When dogs shed, some of their hair falls out. German shepherds shed so much that people call them "German shedders". Brushing them every day helps. But if your family doesn't like dog hair on the couch or rugs, get a dog that doesn't shed. A West Highland terrier might be a better choice.

Okay, signing off for now . . . until the next adventure at Hound Hotel!

Yours very factually,

Alfreeda Wolfe

Glossary

alpha person or animal who is the leader and is the best or most powerful member of a group

annoying making someone feel angry or impatient

boarding kennels place where dogs are kept and cared for while their owners are away

costume clothes worn to dress up as someone or something else

guests people staying in a hotel, a motel, or a bed and breakfast

instinct behaviour that a person or animal is born with rather than learning it

laundry clothes that are being washed or that need to be washed

mutter speak in a low tone with the mouth nearly closed, in a quiet and unclear way

obstacle something that blocks or stands in the way

paddock small fenced-in field where animals can exercise

serious not joking

temper likelihood of becoming angry

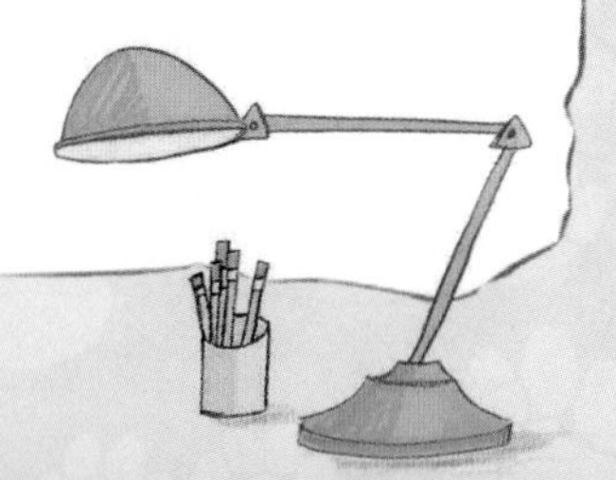

Talk about it

1. Think about a time when you got angry with your sibling or best friend. Did you lose your temper like Alfie? Or did you keep your cool like Crosby? Give examples of your actions.

2. Alfie takes deep breaths to try to control his temper. List three other things you could do to calm yourself when you're angry.

3. On page 68, Alfreeda has shared some facts (and opinions) about German shepherds. Do you think a German shepherd would be a good dog for your family? Why or why not?

Write about it

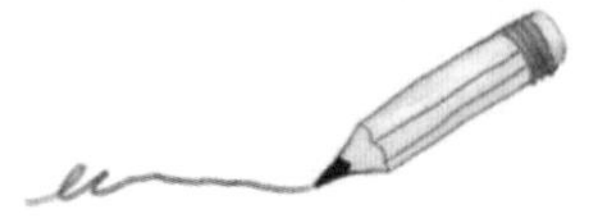

1. Through actions only, Crosby teaches Alfie how to keep his cool. But what if Crosby could talk? What advice would he give? What would he say about Bruno and Alfreeda? Write a short conversation between Crosby and Alfie.

2. Write a letter to the twins' dad about Crosby and Bruno. Use either Alfie's or Alfreeda's point of view.

3. Write a one-page essay on German shepherds. Use at least three sources.

About the author

Shelley Swanson Sateren grew up with five pet dogs: a beagle, a terrier mix, a terrier-poodle mix, a Weimaraner and a German shorthaired pointer. As an adult, she adopted a lively West Highland white terrier called Max. As well as having written many children's books, Shelley has worked as a children's book editor and in a children's bookshop. She lives in Minnesota, USA, with her husband, and has two grown-up sons.

About the illustrator

Deborah Melmon has worked as an illustrator for more than 25 years. After graduating from Academy of Art University in San Francisco, USA, she began her career illustrating covers for a weekly magazine supplement. Since then, she has produced artwork for more than twenty children's books. Her artwork can also be found on wrapping paper, greetings cards and fabric. Deborah lives in California, USA, and shares her studio with an energetic Airedale terrier called Mack.

ADVENTURES AT HOUND HOTEL
Cool Crosby
Shelley Swanson Sateren
Deborah Melmon

ADVENTURES AT HOUND HOTEL
Drooling Dudley
Shelley Swanson Sateren
Deborah Melmon

ADVENTURES AT HOUND HOTEL
Fearless Freddie
Shelley Swanson Sateren
Deborah Melmon

ADVENTURES AT HOUND HOTEL
Growling Gracie
Shelley Swanson Sateren
Deborah Melmon

ADVENTURES AT HOUND HOTEL
Homesick Herbie
Shelley Swanson Sateren
Deborah Melmon

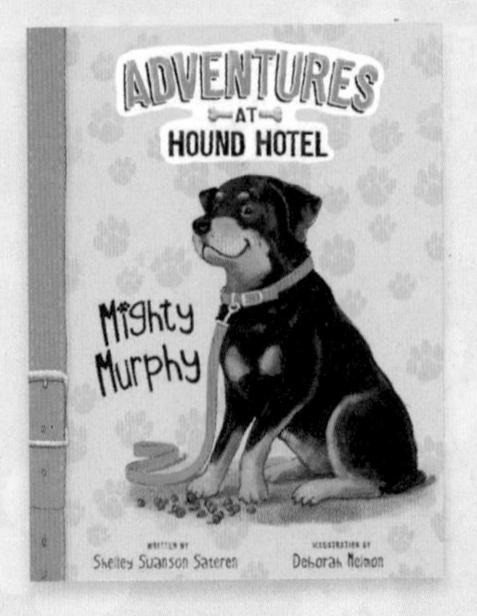
ADVENTURES AT HOUND HOTEL
Mighty Murphy
Shelley Swanson Sateren
Deborah Melmon

ADVENTURES AT HOUND HOTEL
Mudball Molly
Shelley Swanson Sateren
Deborah Melmon

ADVENTURES AT HOUND HOTEL
Stinky Stanley
Shelley Swanson Sateren
Deborah Melmon